The world's best
DAD JOKES
for kids
VOLUME 3

Did you hear the one about...

Every single one
illustrated

SWERLING & LAZAR

Andrews
PUBLIS

D1044482

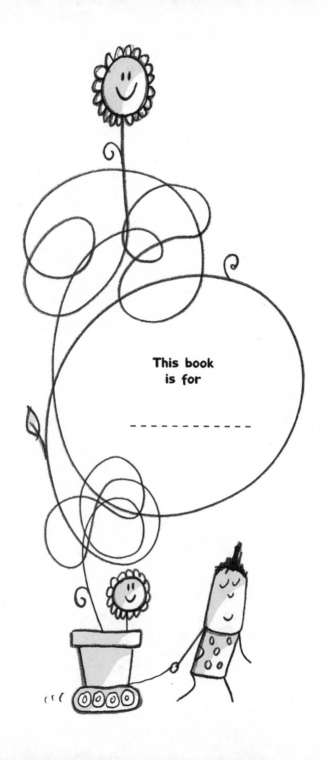

This book
is for

- - - - - - - - - -

What do rabbits use in the shower?

Hare conditioner.

What did the fog say to the boat?

I mist you.

Which country has
lots of dinnerware?

The United Plates of America.

What do you call two
bananas?

A pair of slippers.

What did the computer do to his foot when he lost his shoe?

He rebooted it.

What's a dog's favorite instrument?

A trombone.

What was the bunny's favorite music?

Hip-hop.

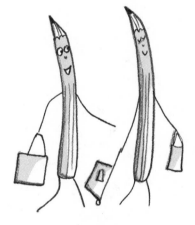

DEPARTURES

Where do pencils spend their vacations?

In Pencilvania.

What do you call a tired pea?

Sleep-pea.

What kind of key opens a banana?

A monkey.

What lights up a sports stadium?

A soccer match.

What happens to spoons that overwork?

They go stir-crazy.

I saw a kidnapping today.

I decided not to wake him up.

When a clown farts . . .

. . . does it smell funny?

If you ever need an ark . . .

. . . I Noah guy.

What do you call a Frenchman in sandals?

Felippe Fallop.

He used to be a banker.

But then he lost interest.

He told a bad chemistry joke.

There was no reaction.

Jokes about German sausages . . .

. . . really are the wurst!

What did the pirate say when he turned 80?

Aye matey.

Sometimes I tuck my knees
into chest and lean forward.

It's just how I roll.

What noise does a nut
make when it sneezes?

CASHEW!

What goes hahahahaHAHAhaha-THUMP?

A monster laughing his head off.

What kind of room can you eat?

 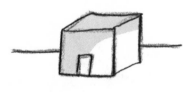

A mushroom.

How do tuna and cod watch the news?

On telefishion.

Which is fastest, cold or heat?

Heat. Because you can catch a cold.

What was the dentist's favorite course in college?

Flossophy.

How does a monster count to 19?

On his fingers.

Doctor doctor, I haven't slept for days!

Why not?

Because I sleep at night.

What do you find in the middle of the ocean?

The letter "e."

Who delivers gifts to dogs on Christmas Eve?

Santa Paws.

She has an addiction to cheddar cheese . . .

. . . but it's only mild.

He used to be afraid of
hurdles . . .

. . . but he got over it.

What do you call
a crocodile with
a new camera?

Happy snappy.

Murphy's Law says anything that can go wrong will go wrong.

Cole's Law is thinly sliced cabbage.

Coleslaw

I'm friends with 25 letters of the alphabet.

I just don't know Y.

How did the rabbit rob the snowman?

He held up his hair dryer and demanded, "Hand over that carrot!"

Why did the kid kick his ball around his backyard?

It was a home game.

What do you call James Bond in the bath?

Bubble O Seven.

If you have 12 eggs in one hand
and 15 apples in the other,
what have you got?

**Weirdly big
hands.**

My brother recently got flattened
by a pile of books.

He's only got his shelf to blame.

Why does a milking stool only have three legs?

Because the cow has the udder.

What do you always get on your birthday?

Another year older.

What do you call
a pack of wolves?

Wolfgang.

Why do cats make great pets?

Because they are purrfect.

What happened after the cat ate the clown fish?

It felt funny.

Why did the painting go to jail?

Because it was framed.

What do you find on a very tiny beach?

Microwaves.

What did the scarf say to the hat?

**You go ahead,
I'll hang around.**

Did you hear about the magic tractor?

FIELD
NEXT
LEFT

**It was just driving along and then
suddenly turned into a field!**

How do cats make coffee?

In a purrcolator.

What do trash collectors eat?

Junk food.

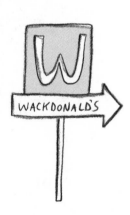

WACKDONALD'S

How did Cinderella's cat get to the ball?

With the help of her Furry Godmother.

What can you always count on?

Your fingers.

Why do rabbits have fur coats?

Because they look silly in leather jackets.

How do you make Anti-freeze?

Send her to the North Pole!

When is the moon not hungry?

When it's full.

What does a cat like
to eat on a hot day?

A mice
cream cone.

Why can't penguins fly?

They can't afford
the airplane tickets!

What wears shoes but has no feet?

A sidewalk.

What sort of stories does a ship captain tell his children?

Ferry tales.

Why is a bride like a telephone?

Both have rings.

What do you call a cat that lives in an igloo?

An eskimew.

What do you call a cheerful bearded man dressed in red, who claps his hands every Christmas?

Santapplause.

What do you call a fish with four eyes?

Fiiiish.

What did the frog order for dinner?

A burger and Diet Croak.

What's big, gray, and
drones on when it talks?

A mumbo
jumbo.

What's hairy and sneezes?

A coconut with a cold.

What do the letter A and a rose have in common?

Bs come after them.

Why was the cat grouchy?

Bad
mewd.

What sits on the seabed and shakes?

A nervous wreck.

How did the cow transport all his stuff?

He rented a mooving truck.

How does a dog stop a movie?

He uses paws.

Why do mice need oiling?

SQUEAK
SQUEAK

Because they squeak.

How do you get rid of varnish?

Take away the R.

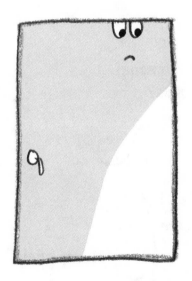

When is a door not a door?

When it's ajar.

If you slice five peaches into five pieces, what do you end up with?

Sticky fingers.

What do you call a camel with three humps?

Humphrey.

How can you make
your money go a
long way?

Put your money in a rocket!

What did the
policemen say
when a spider
crawled down
his back?

You're under
a vest!

What does a cat rest on at night?

A caterpillow.

How do chicks get out of their shells?

They eggs it.

**What do you call
a girl with a frog
on her head?**

Lily.

**Did you hear about the
lazy skeleton?**

He was bone idle.

What do you get if you cross an elephant with a mouse?

A huge hole in the baseboard!

Why was the glowworm disappointed?

The kids weren't all that bright.

What did one toilet say to the other?

You look a bit flushed.

How many police officers did it take to arrest a light bulb?

POLICE STATION

None. It turned itself in.

What's worse than raining cats and dogs?

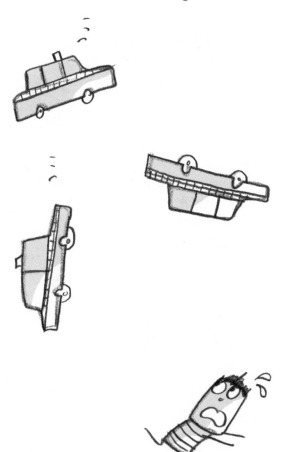

Hailing taxis.

**What do you call a cat
that's swallowed a duck?**

**A duck-filled
fatty-puss.**

**Want to hear
a long joke?**

Joooooooooooooooke.

What do you get when the air-conditioning in a rabbit hole stops working?

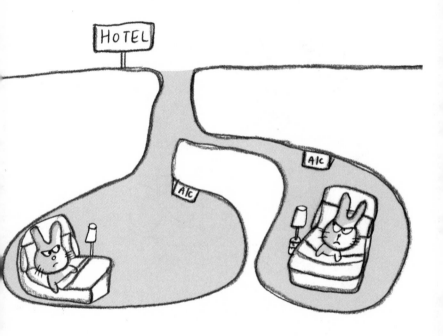

Hot cross bunnies.

What kind of cats are good at bowling?

Alley cats.

Why did Captain Hook cross the road?

To get to the second hand store.

How do you know carrots are good for your eyes?

Have you ever seen a rabbit with a flashlight?

Did you hear about the blacksmith dog?

When anyone shouts at him, he bolts for the door.

What's the difference between elephants and grapes?

Grapes are purple.

ELEPHANT

GRAPE

What's green and goes camping?

A brussels scout.

What is the shiniest fish in the sea?

A starfish.

He didn't like his beard at first . . .

. . . then it grew on him.

The boy gave
away all his
dead batteries.

Free of charge!

My dog Rover used to
chase this kid on a bike,
a lot.

Eventually, I had to
take Rover's bike
away.

Why did the physics teacher break
up with the biology teacher?

There was no
chemistry.

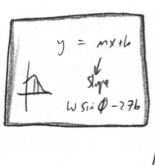

$$y = mx + b$$

slope

$W \sin \phi - 276$

If April showers bring Mayflowers,
what do Mayflowers bring?

Pilgrims.

If you know a really
good fish pun . . .

. . . please let
minnow.

How did the
tree feel in
spring?

Releaved.

Why shouldn't you tell jokes about peanut butter?

People may spread it around.

What's the worst thing about a class on ancient history?

The teacher tends to Babylon.

When my wife asked me to stop
impersonating a flamingo . . .

. . . I really
had to put my
foot down.

What did Cinderella say when
her photos got lost in the mail?

One day my prints
will come . . .

Why did the sea urchin dream of space?

He wanted to be a starfish.

**What's the best thing
about elevator jokes?**

They work on so many levels.

What does even the most careful person overlook?

Their nose.

Where should an 800-pound alien go?

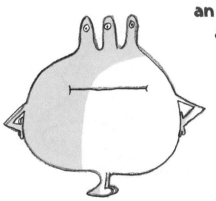

On a diet.

What do you call a boy named Lee who has no one to talk to?

Lonely.

Why do dragons sleep during the day?

So they can fight knights.

What do you get when
you cross a snake
with a pie?

A pie-thon.

Why should you
stand in a corner
if you're cold?

They're 90 degrees.

Did you hear about the mathematician who was afraid of negative numbers?

He'd stop at nothing to avoid them.

-3 -2 -1 0

Where do you learn to make banana splits?

SUNDAE SCHOOL

At sundae school.

What did the tree say to the wind?

Leaf me alone!

How do crazy people go through the forest?

On a psycho path.

What do prisoners use to call each other?

Cell phones.

What never asks questions but is often answered?

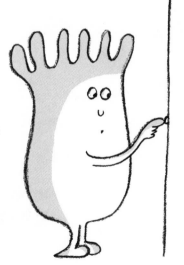

A doorbell.

Why did the cantaloupe jump in the lake?

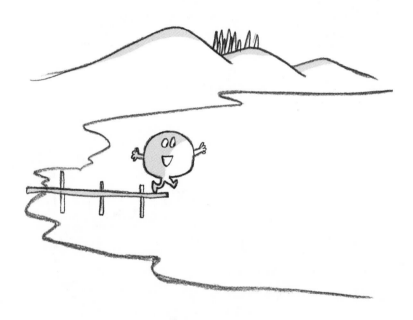

It wanted to be a watermelon.

What kind of insect is difficult to understand?

A mumblebee.

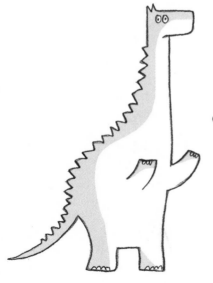

Why can't dinosaurs clap?

Because they're dead.

What's the difference between a school teacher and a train?

One says: "Spit that gum out!" And the other says: "Chew chew! Chew chew!"

What do you call a man with a spade in his head?

Doug.

What's the best time to eat a crispy apple?

At crunch time.

Where do fish keep their savings?

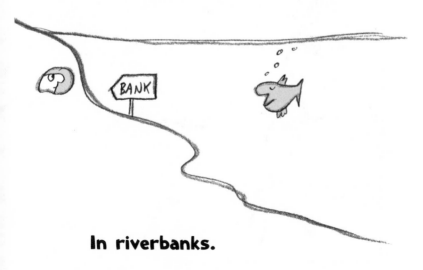

In riverbanks.

Where do you find Mexico?

On a map.

What do you call a one-legged giraffe?

Eileen.

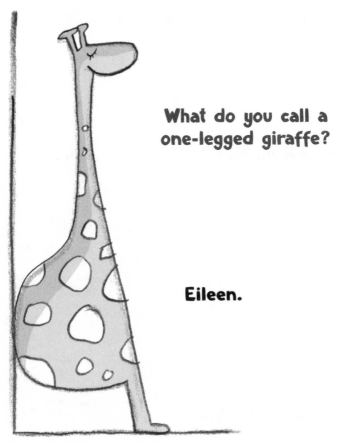

Why was there thunder and lightning in the laboratory?

The scientists were brainstorming.

What's black, red, black, red, black, red, black, red?

A zebra with a sunburn.

Where do insects go shopping?

The flea market.

What did the one candle say to the other?

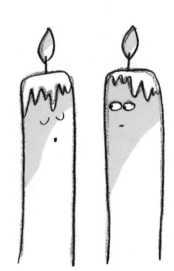

I'm going out tonight.

What do you call a funny mountain?

Hill-arious.

What goes through tunnels and over hills but doesn't move?

A road.

**What happened to the dog
that swallowed a firefly?**

It barked with delight.

**What's small, round, and can't
stop laughing?**

A tickled onion.

What did one penny say
to the other?

We make cents.

Why do moon
rocks taste better
than earth rocks?

Because they're meteor.

Why was the man looking for food on his friend's head?

**Because his friend had said:
"Dinner's on me!"**

Why is Peter Pan always flying?

Because he Neverlands.

Where do you find
an upside-down
tortoise?

**Exactly where
you left it.**

What happened to the duck who
heard a really funny joke?

He totally quacked up.

What snake is good at building houses?

A boa constructor.

What do you get when you mix a cow with a duck?

Milk and quackers.

**Why did the man put his
money in the freezer?**

He wanted cold, hard cash.

Which hand is it better to write with?

Neither, you should write with a pen!

Why did the man go out with a prune?

Because he couldn't find a date.

Why do you go to bed at night?

Because the bed won't come to you.

Were you long in hospital?

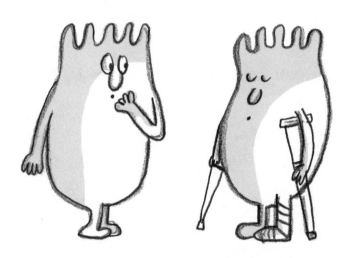

**No, I was the same size
as I am now.**

What's the difference between bird flu and swine flu?

One requires tweetment and the other needs oinkment.

What do you call helping a lemon in trouble?

Lemon-aid.

**What's green and sits
moping in the corner?**

The Incredible Sulk.

I stayed up all night trying
to work out where the
sun was . . .

. . . then it dawned on me.

Where should a 400-pound alien go?

On a diet.

What did the mayonnaise say when the refrigerator door was opened?

Close the door, I'm dressing.

Did you hear about the guy who drank eight giant sodas?

He burped 7-Up.

What did the strict ghost say to his son?

Don't spook unless you're spooken to!

What snake is
3.14 feet long?

A π thon.

Why did seven
eat nine?

Because it's important to eat
three squared meals a day.

How do you get two whales in a car?

Start in England and head west.

Why do pelicans carry fish in their beaks?

Because they haven't got pockets.

What was the tree's favorite drink?

Root beer.

Why aren't koalas actual bears?

They don't have the right koalafications.

Why was the drum so sleepy?

..YAWN

He was beat.

What kind of shoes does a ninja wear?

Sneakers.

What did the paper say to the pencil?

Write on!

ADJECTIVES

What kind of dinosaur makes a brilliant English teacher?

A Thesaurus.

Why do eggs make such good fighter pilots?

Because they can scramble really fast.

I used to have terrible amnesia.

I used to have terrible amnesia.

How can you tell if there is an elephant under your bed?

You smack your head on the ceiling.

Where do werewolves live?

In warehouses.

What do you call a miserable ship?

A woe boat.

Why was the severely allergic woman worried about the weather?

Because it was raining cats and dogs.

Why didn't the cake like to play golf with the donut?

Because he always got a hole in one.

**What has many thousands
of ears but can't hear a thing?**

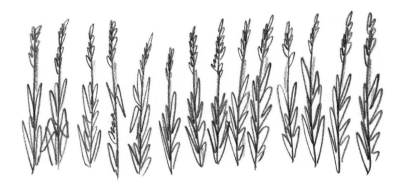

A field of corn.

**What musical
instrument did the
dentist love to play?**

The tuba toothpaste.

Why was the oak tree going to the dentist?

To get a root canal.

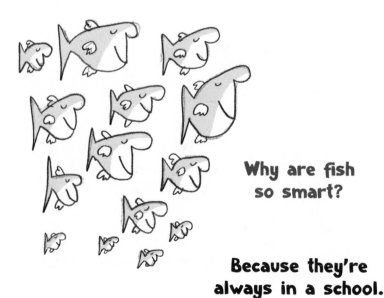

Why are fish so smart?

Because they're always in a school.

Why are horses useless at dancing?

Because they have two left feet.

What's the difference between a television set and a newspaper?

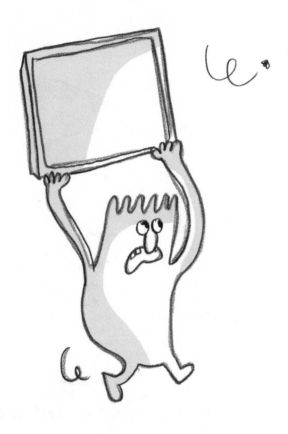

Ever tried to swat a fly with a TV?

Why was the doctor angry with the nurse?

Because he lost his patients.

Why don't oranges win marathons?

They run out of juice.

How do bees get to school?

They take the buzz.

What creepy crawly may you find in your shoe?

A sockroach.

What did the egg
say to the
banana?

Nothing, eggs can't talk!

Why did the scientist's
breath smell so good?

Because he'd eaten an experi-mint.

What do you call two birds in love?

Tweethearts.

What did the apple tree say to the fruit-picker?

Leaf me alone!

Why did the chicken cross the waterpark?

To get to the other slide.

What kind of computers do babies use?

Naptops.

Why did Rudolph the Reindeer go to school?

To learn the elf-abet.

**What do you call
a cow that can't fly?**

Ground beef.

**What's the worst thing
about being alone?**

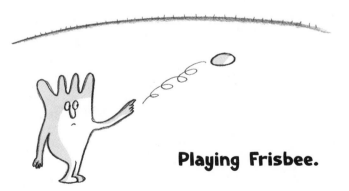

Playing Frisbee.

Why do ducks make the best detectives?

They manage to quack every case.

What kind of tea is hard to swallow?

Reality.

What kind of lion
is no one afraid of?

A dandelion.

Have you laughed aloud at The World's Best Jokes for Kids VOLUMES 1, 2, and 4?

The World's Best Dad Jokes for Kids Volume 3

copyright © 2019 by Lisa Swerling and Ralph Lazar. All rights reserved.
Printed in the United States of America. No part of this book may be used
or reproduced in any manner whatsoever without written permission except
in the case of reprints in the context of reviews.

Andrews McMeel Publishing
a division of Andrews McMeel Universal
1130 Walnut Street, Kansas City, Missouri 64106

www.andrewsmcmeel.com

19 20 21 22 23 VEP 10 9 8 7 6 5 4 3 2 1

ISBN: 978-1-5248-5331-0

Library of Congress Control Number: 2019940388

Made by:
Versa Press Inc.
Address and location of manufacturer:
1465 Spring Bay Road/Route 26
East Peoria, IL 61611
1st Printing—9/9/19

For lots more funny, silly, and random jokes,
visit us online:
www.lastlemon.com/silliness
www.instagram.com/silliness.is
www.facebook.com/silliness.is

Send us a joke. If we like it,
we'll illustrate it:
www.lastlemon.com/silliness/submit

ATTENTION: SCHOOLS AND BUSINESSES

Andrews McMeel books are available at quantity discounts with
bulk purchase for educational, business, or sales promotional use.
For information, please e-mail the Andrews McMeel Publishing
Special Sales Department: specialsales@amuniversal.com.